Mark McGwire
Home Run King

Written by C.A. Piparo
Illustrated by Brian Gregg

ALL-STAR
BOOKS

Infinity Plus One
Ridgewood, New Jersey

For Nani and Papa
—C.A.P.

Printed in U.S.A. 10 9 8 7 6 5 4 3 2 1

On October 1, 1961 Roger Maris broke Babe Ruth's home run record when he slammed his sixty-first homer that season. Exactly two years later, on October 1, 1963, future home–run record breaker Mark McGwire was born in Pomona, CA.

Almost forty years passed without anyone touching Maris's record.

But in the 1998 season, that sixty-first home run was passed by not one, but two amazing players—Mark McGwire and Sammy Sosa.

The St. Louis Cardinals' first baseman, Mark McGwire, was the first man to reach, and pass, the 61 mark.

Mark knew the season was meant to be an exciting one when he hit a grand slam home run on opening day—the first Cardinal to ever do so.

His belief was confirmed when he tied Roger Maris's record of 61 homers on his father's sixty-first birthday.

The next day, on September 8,
1998, Mark broke the record
when he hit home run number 62!
Thanks to the incredible talent and
sportsmanship displayed by Mark
and Sammy Sosa throughout their
home run race, this was quite
possibly the most memorable
baseball season ever.

Mark is the third of five sons.
His parents, John and Ginger,
always encouraged their boys to
play sports.
Mark's father used to be an
amateur boxer, and his mom was
a swimmer in college.
While he was growing up, Mark
liked watching his father work out
with a punching bag in the
garage.

His parents also taught their sons the importance of always trying their hardest.
They asked the boys to be polite and respectful at all times.

When he was seven years old, Mark's dad would not let him join Little League.

He did not like the arguing that always seemed to take place among parents and coaches.

Mark was so upset about not being able to play baseball that he cried for hours.

His father changed his mind the following year. Mark hit his very first home run when he went up to bat for the very first time!

During the next three years, Mark set his town Little League record for home runs.

It was the first of many records that Mark would make or break!

Mark also loved to watch
baseball.
His parents used to take their sons
to see the California Angels
whenever they could.

At home, young Mark would forget about all his other responsibilities while he lay on the floor watching baseball games on television. "Mom, I promise I'll do my chores as soon as the game is over!" he would tell her.

Mark did not have a favorite team or player.

"I'm never going to copy anyone's style," he said. "I'll have my very own way of playing."

Mark's father recognized his son's ability at a young age.
"Son, you have an amazing ability and a natural talent," he told Mark.

When Mark started playing baseball, he was a pitcher.
One day Mark walked so many batters that he started to cry.
"I can't see the plate!" he told his father, who was also the coach.
His father moved him to shortstop for the rest of the game, but Mark still could not see clearly.
A short time later Mark learned that he had extremely poor eyesight. Glasses and eye exercises improved his vision.

Mark played several other sports, including soccer.
He transferred to Damien High School, a Catholic boys school, halfway through his freshman year. He felt it gave him a better opportunity to play sports.

Mark pitched for the junior varsity baseball team and was the starting center on the school's basketball team.

During his sophomore year, Mark
pulled a muscle in his chest.
As a result, he could not swing the
bat well.
He quit the baseball team and
took up golf.

Mark excelled at golf.
That same year, he entered a
tournament.
He tied with another player and
had to play five extra playoff
holes.
Mark beat him on the fifth hole.

As a result of his success in golf,
Mark thought about becoming a
professional golfer.
However, he was soon bored with
the sport.
"It's just not baseball," he often
thought to himself.

Mark could not stay away from
baseball forever.
He returned to the field on the
varsity team in his junior year.

Soon after returning to his favorite sport, Mark began considering a career in professional baseball. Scouts and college coaches from across the country came to see Mark pitch.

They saw his strong arm and
smooth delivery firsthand.
He had an impressive curveball.
The speed of his fastball was over
eighty miles per hour!

Suddenly, near the end of his
senior year, Mark was diagnosed
with appendicitis and
mononucleosis.
He missed the first few weeks of
the season.

When Mark began playing again, his coach started him at first base. He played this position throughout the entire season, and led Claremont to the state playoffs in California.

Mark continued to develop his skill throughout college and broke home run records even then.

Despite Mark's success in college and later in pro ball, there were difficult times to get through.

At one point, after only six years in the Major Leagues, Mark thought his career in baseball was over.

With a little help and the words of his parents echoing in his mind, Mark got through that low point and learned to believe in himself once again.

Now a home run superstar, Mark teaches others what his parents taught him.
Work hard and practice hard.
Always be thankful.
Keep a good attitude.
Mark's good attitude took him far this season!

Mark McGwire will forever be remembered for his achievements in baseball:

- He was the first player to hit more than 50 homers in three consecutive seasons (1996-1998).
- He reached 400 home runs in the fewest at bats in Major League history.
- He played in the All-Star game a whopping ten times.
- He hit 70 home runs in one season!

More importantly, Mark organized his own foundation for abused children. The McGwire Fund for Children donates one million dollars from his salary each year toward helping children.

These achievements, like Mark McGwire's strength of character, are immeasurable.